ANIMAL PLANET
Adventures

Zoo Camp Puzzle

Gail Herman

Illustrated by Bryan Langdo

ZOO CAMP PUZZLE

Published by Liberty Street,
an imprint of Time Inc. Books
225 Liberty Street
New York, New York 10281

LIBERTY
STREET

LIBERTY STREET is a trademark of Time Inc.

Softcover edition
ISBN: 978-1-68330-772-3

First edition, 2017
1 QGT 17
10 9 8 7 6 5 4 3 2 1

Produced by Scout Books & Media Inc

Time Inc. Books products may be purchased for business or promotional
use. For information on bulk purchases, please contact Christi Crowley
in the Special Sales Department at (845) 895-9858.

We welcome your comments and suggestions about Time Inc. Books.
Please write to us at:
Time Inc. Books
Attention: Book Editors
P.O. Box 62310, Tampa, FL 33662–2310
(800) 765-6400

timeincbooks.com

Zoo Camp Puzzle

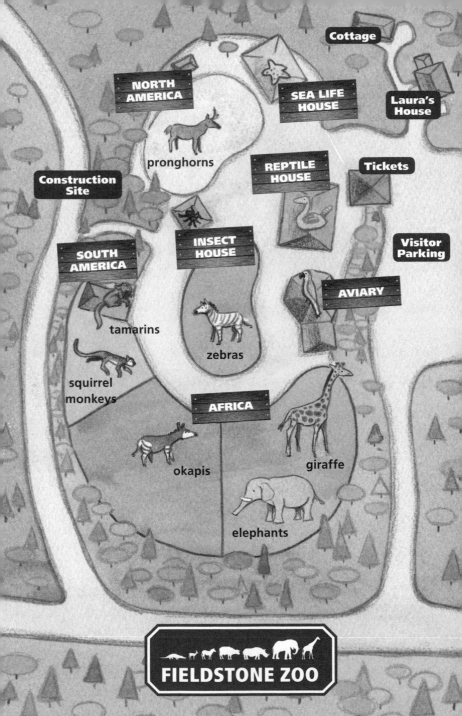

Welcome to the Zoo

A dusty blue minivan pulled into the driveway of Fieldstone Zoo. A big sign on the gate read "CLOSED." Newspaper pages blew across the gravel on the pavement. The place looked empty and forgotten.

Inside the minivan was the Scott family. Mrs. Scott was in the driver's seat. Mr. Scott sat next to her. Ten-year-old twins Rosie and Ava were in the middle row along with Ethan, fifteen. The back of their minivan was stuffed with suitcases and boxes. The Scotts were coming to Iowa from Chicago. But it was just for the spring. They were going to stay here at the Fieldstone Zoo. Mrs. Scott was writing a book on the ways people and animals are alike. She'd been invited to live on the grounds while she worked. She would give author talks about the subject to visitors, too.

Ethan slunk low in his seat. His frown deepened. He didn't say a word. But his feelings were clear. He didn't want to be here.

Rosie fidgeted restlessly. "This is such a bad idea," she complained. "We're leaving our apartment! Our friends!

Why would we want to live at a zoo? We're not even allowed to have pets in our building at home. Now we'll be surrounded by wild animals. It's so unfair! Right, Ava?"

Ava nodded in agreement. "It is unfair. We'll miss school, too," she said quietly.

"You won't be missing anything," Mr. Scott said.

Mr. Scott was a teacher. He was going to homeschool all three children. "We have zoo camp. It starts tomorrow, and it will be fun!" Mr. Scott's voice rose with excitement. He was running the camp during spring vacation. He glanced at Ethan. "And none of you are too old for camp."

WILD AT THE ZOO

The word *zoo* comes from *zoology*, a Greek word that means "animal study." The first known zoo dates back more than 5,000 years, to ancient Egypt. The oldest zoos in the United States, founded more than 100 years ago, are in Boston, New York, Philadelphia, and Chicago. Modern zoos exhibit animals and also work to help preserve animal populations in the wild and teach about animal conservation.

"It's not enough to keep animals in exhibits just for people to look at. There has to be a higher purpose. And for us, it's conservation of species in the wild."
—Jim Breheny, Director of the Bronx Zoo

A BRONX TALE

In 2009, the tiny Kihansi spray toad was in trouble. Named for the place it lived in Tanzania, Africa, its home had been altered by a building project that helped bring electricity to people. The Bronx Zoo and the Toledo Zoo helped save the species through conservation and breeding efforts. More than 2,000 spray toads have been returned to the wild, and a local group in Tanzania is working to help the toads survive and thrive again.

Kihansi spray toad

Ethan let out a groan. He pulled his sweatshirt hood over his head. Maybe this was just a bad dream and he'd be home with his friends in Chicago when he woke up.

"Zoo camp is not the same as school, Dad," Rosie argued. "It will just be us. Bo-ring!"

"Hush," Mrs. Scott said. "Laura said to meet here at ten sharp." The minivan clock read 10:03. "Let's be quiet and sit tight."

The Scotts waited for five minutes. Then ten minutes. Then fifteen. Mr. Scott tapped his foot. He liked people to be on time. And he didn't like surprises.

More minutes ticked by.

"Finally!" Mr. Scott exclaimed,

pointing to a figure hurrying down the driveway toward the car.

Rosie popped the door open and jumped out of the car. "C'mon," she said, as the others followed more slowly.

"Hello! I'm sorry I'm late!" the woman called out. "I'm Laura. Welcome to my zoo!" She shook everyone's hand. Then she smoothed her messy hair and caught her breath. "Somehow the morning got away from me. It usually does."

Laura looked at Rosie and Ava and smiled. "Oh my! I didn't know you were identical twins. How will I tell you apart?"

The twins both wore their curly hair short. But Rosie had on a bright flowered shirt and matching pink jeans. Ava wore a blue shirt and dark blue leggings.

Rosie piped up quickly, answering for both of them. "I'm Rosie, and I wear bright colors. Ava likes darker ones. And she *always* wears two little puff pigtails."

"Well, that's easy then." Laura smiled. The twins exchanged smiles. Laura seemed scattered, but nice.

"You must be Ethan," she said. He pushed his hood off his head and nodded.

"Let me give you all a tour of the zoo," she continued.

Mrs. Scott said, "Maybe we should unpack and—"

"Oh, that can wait," Laura said airily. "I'll be quick—I have an important meeting to get to this afternoon."

FIND THE ANIMALS

In zoos, animals are often grouped together in areas that reflect where and how they live in the wild.

BIOMES are defined by their plant life and climate. Desert tortoises, armadillos, cobras, and kangaroos all live in different places on Earth. But they all live in the desert biome. Animals in a biome exhibit are housed near other animals that live in that biome. Deserts, rainforests, and savannas are examples of biomes.

Desert.

HABITATS are specific places where animals live. A coral reef habitat might include clown fish, octopuses, moray eels, rays, and sharks. Animals that make their homes in and around coral reef habitats may be housed together in an aquarium exhibit.

Coral reef

The Tour

Laura led the family around the small zoo. They approached a row of small buildings. Two zookeepers were hurrying into one, carrying hoses and other equipment.

"That's our Sea Life House," Laura said, waving to the men. "Joe and Luis are trying to fix the touch tank. There's a major leak." She frowned. "I'll introduce you later, when they're not so busy."

Then, urging everyone forward, she led them through the Reptile House.

The twins caught sight of snakes, lizards, and a huge giant tortoise.

"That's way bigger than Hermie," Rosie whispered to Ava. Hermie was Rosie's classroom pet tortoise. The group next visited the Aviary and saw bright-eyed owls, creepy-looking vultures, colorful parrots, and peacocks.

"Now on to the large animal enclosures," said Laura. "First I'll take you to the 'Africa' section."

The enclosures took up a few acres of land. One stretched far into the distance. "That's for our elephants and giraffes. They need a lot of room to move about," Laura explained. "Both sets of animals have their own sheltered areas, too."

Three elephants
walked slowly around
the enclosure, swinging
their trunks.

"They're huge!" Rosie cried.

"Elephants form strong family bonds, just like ours," Mrs. Scott told the children.

"That's right," Laura confirmed.

Two giraffes nibbled on leaves at the tops of trees.

ANIMALS OF THE AFRICAN SAVANNA

Elephants, giraffes, and zebras are just a few of the animals that live in the grasslands. Here are some others that make their home there, too.

The **RHINO** is named for its horn—rhinoceros means "nose-horn" in Greek. These animals are happy on their own, love to wallow in mud to cool off, and only eat plants. Males can weigh more than two tons (4,000 pounds), so they eat a lot of veggies!

Zoo Fact

ROAR!

A lion may be called "King of the Jungle," but it makes its home on the African savanna. Lions live in groups called prides, with as many as 35 in the community. The females hunt and raise the cubs, and the males guard the pride and their territory.

One of the biggest antelopes is called the **WILDEBEEST** or gnu (pronounced "new"). It's one of the strangest-looking ones, too, with a boxy head, curved horns, and a mane. They're noisy animals that grunt and snort. More than one million gnus migrate throughout the year.

"This is hard to believe when you look at them," said Mrs. Scott, "but giraffes have the same number of neck bones as we do—seven. Theirs are super big, though."

"Right again," Laura said, striding away. The family followed her to another enclosure. Here, zebras grazed quietly in a large grassy space. They moved lazily from spot to spot. Their furry ears stood straight up.

"We're going to talk about zebras at zoo camp. Their stripes and patterns, behavior, and traits—so many fascinating facts," Mr. Scott said enthusiastically. Ethan pulled his hood up again and rolled his eyes.

Nearby, in the 'South America' area,

a group of squirrel monkeys chattered to one another. They climbed up and down trees.

"Squirrel monkeys live in groups called troops," Mrs. Scott said. "They talk and play and are really quite social." She smiled at the twins. "Sort of like your scouting troop." The girls nodded.

"Notice their dark-colored muzzles," Laura added.

Ava pointed to a monkey scampering across a branch. "That one looks like Little Mikey's messy face after he eats chocolate chip cookies."

Little Mikey was their cousin.

The monkey plucked a twig from a branch. He held it with two hands and nibbled at it. Rosie stepped closer. "That's how I eat corn on the cob."

Mrs. Scott squeezed Rosie's hand. "That's another trait you share."

Rosie wanted to see everything at once. She hopped from watching the squirrel monkeys to watching the zebras. Then she went back to the monkeys again.

"I'm going all the way from South America to Africa!" she joked. "The animals are all amazing. I can't wait to message my friends and tell them about each one."

Ava stood quietly between her parents, turning in a full circle to watch all the animals intently. She seemed to be memorizing every elephant's wrinkle, every zebra's stripe, every pair of eyes. She grinned at Rosie. She was excited about the animals, too.

"The zoo opens tomorrow," Laura told Mr. and Mrs. Scott. "We were closed for the winter and I'm eager to open up."

"That must be hard, being closed for a whole season," Mr. Scott said. "I'm excited we're here at the start of the new one."

Laura shook her head. "We had a bad year last year and we have to do better this year. We need more visitors. If not, I may have to shut down the zoo altogether."

"Oh no!" Rosie was surprised "You mean close for good?"

Laura nodded.

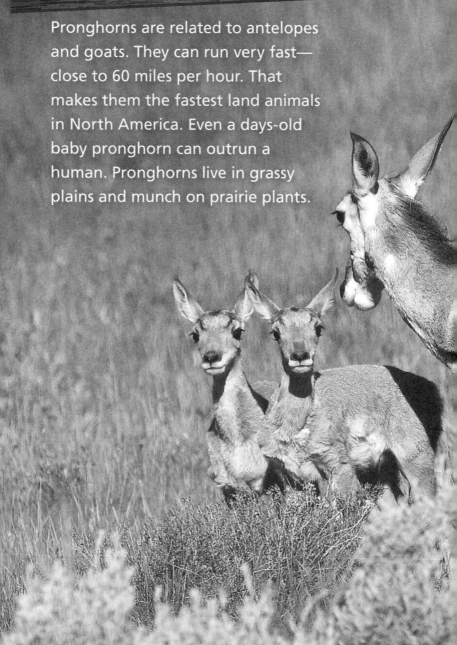

Pronghorns are related to antelopes and goats. They can run very fast— close to 60 miles per hour. That makes them the fastest land animals in North America. Even a days-old baby pronghorn can outrun a human. Pronghorns live in grassy plains and munch on prairie plants.

BOTTOMS UP!
Pronghorns communicate with their bottoms! They raise the big white patches of hair to warn others of danger nearby.

Zoo Fact

"I had no idea the zoo was having problems," said Mrs. Scott.

"I didn't realize how bad it was until we started preparing for the new season. So many expenses, so much to do," Laura admitted. "But I have big plans. Let me show you."

She led the family to the last enclosure, in the North American region. More four-legged animals bounded here and there. They had big patches of white fur and horns.

"Are they antelopes?" Ethan asked.

Rosie nudged him. Ethan sounded suddenly interested. Maybe he was getting excited about the zoo.

Laura shook her head. "Some people call them antelopes. They act like antelopes, too. But they are pronghorns. They can run fast, and they can jump straight up in the air. That's called *pronking*. Some kinds are endangered."

"That's sad," Ava said softly.

"Yes," Laura agreed. "But one pronghorn here is going to have a baby. Actually, the veterinarian thinks there may be twins—and it may happen tomorrow."

"Yeah! Twins!" Ava exclaimed, while Rosie clapped excitedly.

"I called the local newspaper and TV station to cover the event," Laura continued. "It will be great publicity. That's just one of my ideas to bring in visitors."

"Sounds good," Mrs. Scott agreed.

"Are there ways we can help?"

"Yes! You're one of my other ideas," Laura said, pointing at Mrs. Scott. "Hopefully, people who know and love your books will come hear you speak." Then she turned to Mr. Scott. "And our brand-new zoo camp should attract more families. But no pressure," Laura added, smiling. "Now let me show you where you'll be staying."

"*Our* enclosure," Rosie said with a giggle.

Puzzle Solving

Moments later, the Scott family stood outside a bright yellow cottage.

"Our new home," said Mrs. Scott. The family walked around checking out all the rooms.

"It's cute," Rosie declared.

"Can Rosie and I share a room?" asked Ava.

"You bet," said Mr. Scott. "Now, there's a lot to do. Let's go over my system." Rosie and Ava laughed. Even

Ethan grinned a little bit. Their dad always had a system.

Everyone brought in boxes. Each one had a number written on it. Mr. Scott had made a chart listing each one and where it should go. He handed out copies of the chart. Ava glanced at one box: #9. She scanned the chart. "Box #9 goes in the linen closet," she announced.

"That's down the hall," Mrs. Scott said, pointing.

When the car was empty, Rosie skipped into the corner room. It had two big windows and two beds. "Do you like this room, Ava?" she sang out.

Ava slipped inside and smiled. "It's perfect."

Ethan chose a room across the hall. Mr. and Mrs. Scott set up the kitchen. The girls and Ethan unpacked their clothes and other belongings.

"Lunch!" Mrs. Scott called. The family was midway through the platter of sandwiches at the kitchen table when the phone by the sink rang.

Mrs. Scott put the phone on speaker. "Hello?"

"There's been a mix-up," Laura said quickly. "I ordered supplies that we need for tomorrow. But the company called to say their truck broke down and I have to pick them up. I'll be gone all afternoon. Joe and Luis are here, though. They'll take care of the animals. They'll be checking the mother

WHO WORKS AT THE ZOO?

KEEPERS feed and care for animals, making sure they stay active and healthy. They look out for signs of illness. And they take care of their exhibits, too.

This baby elephant measures up as healthy and growing.

A tortoise that isn't feeling well gets a report for the vet.

VETERINARIANS give checkups, prescribe medicine, perform surgeries, and watch over births.

Say **"ahh!" It's** chameleon checkup time.

EDUCATORS teach visitors about animals and conservation.

Say **"Hi!" to** this furry chinchilla.

Other zoo staff work **BEHIND THE SCENES** to build enclosures, prepare food for the animals, and much more.

Exhibits resemble an animal's habitat in the wild.

pronghorn every hour to make sure she's okay."

"Um, what should we—" Mrs. Scott started to say.

"There's a town board meeting about to take place at Town Hall," Laura rushed onward. "We need the board's okay to run the zoo camp. They are supposed to issue a permit today. But someone has to be at the meeting, and I can't be in both places. I called and told them you and your husband would attend for me. If you leave right away, you can just make it. I'll text you the address."

Without waiting for an answer, she hung up.

Mr. Scott strode back and forth across the kitchen, frowning. Mrs. Scott said, "You look just like an anxious lion, pacing back and forth."

Mr. Scott didn't say anything as he hurried out of the room. When he came back, he held out a bunch of papers toward Ethan.

"What's all that?" Ethan asked.

"These are puzzles for the campers," Mr. Scott answered. "They're all about animals at the zoo. I was going to check the puzzles this afternoon. But now I don't have time, so you guys will have to solve them for me." As Ethan took the papers, Mr. Scott added, "Make sure they work. I don't want to hear from you until you've checked them all. This is important!"

Rosie liked puzzles. But she liked

lunch, too. "Now?" she whined.

"Finish your lunch," Mr. Scott said, his voice softening, "then take the puzzles and look around the zoo to figure out the answers. That's what I plan to do with the campers." He took a deep breath. "And, Ethan, keep an eye on the twins," he instructed sternly as he and Mrs. Scott hurried out.

Ava and Rosie gulped their sandwiches. Minutes later, all three siblings headed outside. Ethan read the instructions for the first set of puzzles. "Unscramble the animal names. Hint: they all live in South America."

The siblings followed signs to the South America habitat. They looked over the puzzles.

Scrambled Words

Unscramble the animal names.
Hint: They all live in South America.

Unscramble #1:

QUELSIRR NOMYEK

_ _ _ _ _ _ _ _   _ _ _ _ _ _

YCARPEC

_ _ _ _ _ _ _

Unscramble #2:

BAPYCARA

_ _ _ _ _ _ _ _

CHILLACHIN

_ _ _ _ _ _ _ _ _ _

Unscramble #3:

ROSERHINOC TEEBLE

_ _ _ _ _ _ _ _ _ _   _ _ _ _ _ _

TULANARAT

_ _ _ _ _ _ _ _

"Hey, guys," Ava called suddenly. She stopped in front of the monkey space. "I know the first answer," she exclaimed, pointing to signs on the enclosure.

"What is it?" asked Ethan, staring down at the papers in his hand.

"It must be *squirrel monkey*," she answered.

Ethan checked off the letters on the puzzle sheet. "Good job, Ava," he said.

"Nice!" said Rosie before she raced ahead to a large penned-in area. "Hey! These guys look like small brown pigs."

Ethan looked over her shoulder. "They do look like pigs. But the sign says they're peccaries," he said.

Rosie stared at the second puzzle,

then checked the sign. "That's it!" she cried. "The second answer is *peccary*."

"And these animals look like giant guinea pigs!" Ava added quietly, walking over to a hutch.

"Hey! They're the answer to the next puzzle," Ethan said, scanning the other signs. "*Capybara*."

"And a *chinchilla*!" Ava pointed at an adorable animal that looked a little like a squirrel. "That's in the puzzle, too."

Ethan filled in the answers, and they all headed inside the Insect House.

"Ugh! Do we have to look at these creepy-crawlies?" Rosie groaned, edging away from large plant-filled tanks with insects.

PUZZLED ABOUT PUZZLES?

When you're trying to solve a puzzle, always work in pencil. That way you can erase your answer and try again.

- Crosswords: Read through the clues and write in answers you know right away. Then use those letters to help you figure out tougher clues.

- Word Search: Find an "unusual" letter in the word, like an X or a Q. Then search around that letter, looking up, down, and side to side.

- Unscramble: Look for letters that could go together, like "st" or "qu." Try writing letters in a different order, for a new way of looking at the puzzle.

- Rebus: Write down each answer in full, then add or cross off letters as you go through the clues.

"Yes, they may be answers," Ava said seriously. She moved closer. "That one has a horn, just like a rhinoceros."

"That must be why it's called a *rhinoceros beetle*," Ethan said, reading the sign. "That's the answer to a puzzle."

"And these big hairy spiders!" Rosie exclaimed, almost forgetting her fear. "They're tarantulas! Is that an answer, too?"

"It's a match!" Ava said, writing in *tarantula*.

"We're doing great so far, guys!" said Ethan. He turned to the next page. "There's a bonus puzzle," he said. "But to answer it we have to move on to Africa."

Rosie ran to the Africa enclosures and moved from gate to gate, checking out the animal name signs. "*Okapi*!" she cried out.

"Copy what?" Ethan asked as he and Ava joined her.

"O-KA-PI," Rosie said slowly, pointing to the pen for the animals that looked a bit like zebras and a bit like giraffes.

"I'm right! I'm right!" Rosie tapped on the okapi sign on the enclosure.

"Okay. But where are the animals?" Ava asked.

"That's weird," Rosie said. "The enclosure looks empty. There were a bunch of okapis here when we had the tour."

Ethan shrugged. "Maybe Laura moved them."

The three stood there for a moment, uncertain what to do next.

Then Ethan's phone buzzed.

CHAPTER 4

Missing Animals

"It's from Dad," Ethan said. He turned the screen so the twins could see the text message, too.

PERMIT MEETING ABOUT TO START . . . HOW ARE YOU DOING WITH THE PUZZLES? THERE ARE MORE IN MY BRIEFCASE. DO THOSE, TOO!

"Uh oh," said Ava. She frowned, concerned about her dad. "All caps. He's really worried. What are you going to tell him?"

Ethan just texted his father: OK!

"So what are we waiting for?" Rosie tapped her foot impatiently. "Let's get moving!"

"Slow down," Ethan told Rosie. "Let's finish these puzzles first. Then we can get the others from Dad's briefcase." He turned to the next page. "The next puzzle is a word search: Animals at Our Zoo. It says here, 'All these animals live at the zoo here. Begin at the Reptile House, then go to the Africa area, and finally to the South America habitat.'"

The three followed arrows to all three regions, circling names in the word search as they went.

Animals at Our Zoo
Word Search

```
A X G R L A X O F T F I O T D
A L H I R C E W N M I P Z A Z
R W L B R G E A O T G A R M V
A E E I W A H G T T A K I A E
B Z D S H P F P Q R O O O R L
Y F W I E C S F T F N D B I Q
P H I L P W N J E U E E U N L
A E E F Z S A I E Y E K N O M
C M C N L L Z P H T G H U D V
T O R T O I S E L C B C U K B
I D R A Z I L E P M F S S V T
```

REPTILE HOUSE	SOUTH AMERICA	AFRICA
LIZARD	BEETLE	ELEPHANT
TORTOISE	CAPYBARA	GIRAFFE
	CHINCHILLA	OKAPI
	MONKEY	ZEBRA
	SPIDER	

"Wait, there's more." Rosie said when they'd gotten every answer. "Secret Bonus," she read out loud. "One type of animal in the puzzle isn't on the list. Hint: It starts with 'T' and is in the rain forest."

Secret Bonus Word

T _ _ _ _ _ _

"South America has rain forests," said Ethan. "I think we're in the right place."

"T . . . T . . . What can it be?" Rosie muttered, as they looked around.

Ava stopped at one enclosure sign. "Tamarins live here," she called out. "They're another kind of monkey. Do you think that's the animal in the puzzle?"

MEET THE TAMARINS

Tamarins are small monkeys that live in the South American rain forest. About the size of squirrels, they are good at racing up and down trees. They use their long tails for balance. Many species are endangered, and some zoos have special conservation programs that help increase their populations in the wild. Tamarin species are often named for their distinctive looks.

BROWN-MANTLED tamarins are named for their brown upper bodies (a mantle is a cape or shawl that wraps around the shoulders).

The **COTTON TOP** has long white fur from the top of its head to its shoulders.

The **EMPEROR** has a long white moustache (it resembles a famous German emperor, Wilhelm II).

Can you guess why this is called a **RED-HANDED** tamarin?

The **GOLDEN LION** has a lionlike mane and yellow fur.

Zoo Fact

IT TAKES TWO

A female tamarin usually has twins, and both parents share child-rearing tasks. For example, the father carries the babies on his back most of the time. Older siblings pitch in, too!

The three huddled over the puzzle, picking out the right letters. "Yes!" Ethan exclaimed and wrote *tamarin* at the bottom of the list.

"That's funny," Ava said. "This enclosure is also empty . . ." They all looked up.

"Just like the okapis," Rosie finished.

"Hmm," said Ethan. "More missing animals." He frowned. "Maybe moving the animals around is one of the changes Laura talked about."

B-z-z-z! B-z-z-z! Ethan's phone sounded. "Dad again," he said. "Another text message. And more caps."

DID YOU FIND THE OTHER PUZZLES? NO CELL PHONES ALLOWED DURING PERMIT

ZOO-TRITION

Zoo staffers work hard to feed each animal the best way, making sure they get the nutrition they need. They try to make the experience as natural as possible, placing food where it would be in the wild. And during hot weather, animals may get frozen treats to keep them cool.

Food is placed up high for long-necked **GIRAFFES**.

Meals are hung where **TIGERS** can jump and pounce on food.

LEMURS dig for food hidden inside a Halloween pumpkin.

Frozen food is a summertime treat for a **POLAR BEAR**.

MEETING—WILL CHECK BACK LATER.

Ethan didn't want to get his father more stressed out. So he just texted back: NO WORRIES! He knew he had to go find those puzzles.

CHAPTER 5

Strange Happenings

"Listen," Ethan told the twins, "Dad's super anxious about getting the puzzles checked. I have to go back to the cottage and get those other ones now." The girls nodded.

"It won't take long. I'll meet you by the zebra enclosure. It's just down this path," he instructed.

Already, Rosie was off and running. She pulled Ava behind her.

"Wait for me there," Ethan called,

trying to sound grown up and in charge. "And do the next puzzle, the animal crossword."

Ava and Rosie walked slowly to the zebra enclosure. They worked on the crossword puzzle together. "I know 6 down!" Rosie clapped. "I'll give you a hint, Ava. It starts with 'T.' "

"Thanks. Got it!" Ava scribbled in the answer. Soon they figured out the other clues. *That didn't take long,* Ava thought as she gazed at the zebras. They were running around and around the grassy circle. But they seemed different than this morning. *They're running so fast,* she thought. *They look upset.* She headed over to Rosie, who was now watching the squirrel monkey

Fun Facts Crossword

Across

2. This animal eats leaves from treetops.
7. Monkeys ________ bananas before they eat them.
8. Every zebra has its own pattern of _________.

Down

1. Snakes can't _________. They don't have eyelids.
3. The ostrich is a bird. But it can't _________.
4. The largest land animal in the world is an ___________.
5. This bird can turn its head almost all the way around.
6. Like some turtles, a ___________ can live more than 100 years.

that looked like Little Mikey.

The look-alike monkey moved closer to the girls. He crouched by the glass. He rocked back and forth. Then he stopped. Suddenly, he hit the viewing window.

Bang bang! Bang bang!

Ava and Rosie jumped back, startled.

The monkey bared his teeth and grunted angrily.

"That's scary," Rosie said to Ava. "He was so nice and happy this morning."

"I know," Ava agreed. "The zebras were happy and calm, too. But look at them now. They seem upset about something. What do you think is wrong?"

"I don't know." Rosie shook her head. "But when I'm upset, I feel like moving, too. Remember that time at camp?"

RAIN FOREST ANIMALS

Rain forests occur around the world. Some, such as the Amazon rain forest, are warm and humid. Others, such as those on the Pacific northwest of the U.S., are cool and damp. Rain forests cover just 6% of Earth's surface yet are home to about 50% of all wildlife. Each has four levels. Let's explore who lives where.

Black-mantled howler monkey

Silky pygmy anteater

Titan beetle

Emerald tree boa

Fruit bat

Tarsier

Army ant

Cassowary

Ocelot

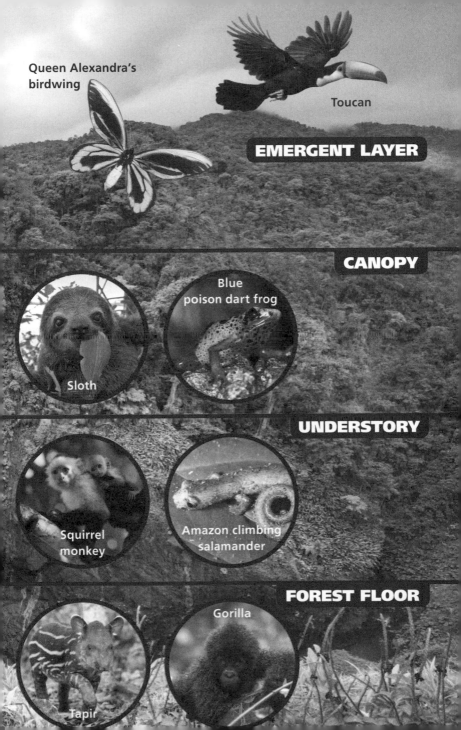

Queen Alexandra's birdwing

Toucan

EMERGENT LAYER

CANOPY

Blue poison dart frog

Sloth

UNDERSTORY

Squirrel monkey

Amazon climbing salamander

FOREST FLOOR

Gorilla

Tapir

Rosie kept talking, running from spot to spot to act out her story. "And I couldn't settle down," she said "until . . ."

Suddenly, she trailed off, stopping short by the zebra gate.

"Until what?" Ava asked.

"Huh?" Rosie said, forgetting her story. "Look here."

She pointed to the gate. The lock was scraped. Deep scratches ran from side to side. Then she and Ava curiously went to examine the squirrel monkeys' enclosure. That fence had deep grooves, too.

"That's strange," Rosie said. "The grooves in the fence around the monkey area look like they were just made—the wood is so much lighter. I bet you would have noticed them when we were here earlier—you notice everything!"

"I'm not sure," Ava said thoughtfully. "I was looking at the animals, not the fences."

"I wonder if these marks mean something. Do you think—?"

Suddenly, the twins heard loud voices in the distance. Joe and Luis were on the other side of the zoo, busy fixing the leaky tank, so it probably wasn't them. So to whom did the voices belong? And what were they doing here?

"Let's check it out," Rosie said curiously, and began running in the direction of the woods that edged the zoo.

"Stop!" Ava called out to her sister. "Ethan said we should meet him by the—" But Rosie was gone.

CHAPTER 6

Where Are the Animals?

"Rosie!" Ava hurried after her sister. "We just can't leave. Ethan told us to go to the zebras."

Rosie called back to her sister, "I'll be right back." Then she continued sprinting toward the trees.

"Wait," Ava called. "I'm coming, too."

By now, Rosie was far ahead. Ava could barely make out her sister's bright flowered top. She ran as quickly as she could to catch up.

At the end of the path, Ava passed the pronghorn enclosure. She skidded to a stop and stared. That enclosure was empty, too. But Ava didn't have time to think about that now. She needed to stay with Rosie, so she took off again.

Seconds later, Ava reached the woods. Bare trees bent in the wind. They looked spooky against the darkening afternoon sky. Ava shivered, but she kept going.

Midway through the trees, she caught up to Rosie. Out of breath, panting, Ava said, "I have something to tell you . . . The pronghorns—"

"Look," said Rosie, interrupting. "If you squint, you can see some people over there."

A BUSY DAY

The day starts early at the zoo. There's a lot for the keepers to do—and the animals, too.

Brush! Brush! Healthy teeth help camels eat lots of grasses and vegetation.

Playtime! Keeping animals active means giving them activities to do. This hippo mom and baby are having bubble-icious fun.

Checkup! This baby macaw is getting weighed to make sure it's growing at a healthy rate.

Yum! Mealtime means special foods are prepared for each animal.

Naptime! After a long day, this red panda catches up on its sleep.

A zookeeper counts the squirrel monkeys. How many do you see?

Ava peered through the trees and branches, looking in the direction her sister pointed. She could make out a low fence behind a line of trees. Beyond that, she saw the backs of three men. They moved hurriedly. Nearby, a truck idled. One man tossed a big object inside.

"I can't really see much. Can you figure out what they are doing?" Ava whispered.

"No. Let's get closer."

They moved toward the fence by the trees. A strong gust of wind blew. The trees swayed and the leaves rustled. The voices were louder now, but Rosie and Ava could hear only bits of conversation.

"Equipment . . . packed up . . ."

"Night job . . ."

"Come back for more later . . ."

"Bigger truck . . ."

"Better drills . . ."

Suddenly, the truck sprang to life with a low humming sound. The men jumped inside. Then they were gone and the woods were quiet again.

HAVE YOU HERD?

Herds and troops are two of the names given to families and large groups of animals. Elephants have strong family bonds within their herds, and older sisters babysit their baby siblings. Baboons live in troops of varying sizes, from about a dozen to more than 100. They use different sounds and facial expressions to communicate with one another. Here are some other animal groups.

Zoo Fact

JUST HANGING OUT

Capybaras are social animals, but there's no special word to describe them. They don't care—they're happy hanging out together.

Chimpanzees form **COMMUNITIES**, with up to 100 members.

Prairie dogs live in underground burrows called **TOWNS**.

A meerkat **MOB** is a family group that can include 20 or more members.

Ava glanced at her sister. "That was weird," she said. "I wonder what they were talking about."

Rosie didn't answer. She was thinking so hard, she was strangely silent. "What were you saying about the pronghorns?" she finally asked.

"I think they're missing, too," Ava said. "I passed their enclosure—and it was empty."

Rosie was still quiet, so Ava spoke up. "We've got to go back," she said. "We're supposed to meet Ethan by the zebras."

"Wait! I just realized something—"

"Rosie, we have to hurry. You can tell Ethan and me when we get back," Ava said.

The sisters raced toward the zebra place. They reached the enclosure just as Ethan arrived from the other direction.

"Ethan," Rosie blurted. "The okapis! The tamarins! They're all missing."

"And the pronghorns, too," added Ava.

"Something strange is happening. Something is wrong. I think the animals have been stolen!" Rosie cried.

Animal Thieves

"**S**tolen? Rosie, what are you talking about?" Ava asked, her eyes widening with concern.

Ethan looked confused. "Go ahead, Rosie. Tell us," Ethan said.

Rosie began, "Okay. Those men—"

"What men?" Ethan said.

"We saw them on the road," Ava explained.

"You . . . you were by the road?" Ethan spluttered, his face turning red. "You were supposed to stay here!"

BEING A WILDLIFE VET

Zoo vets go to veterinary medicine school after college. They pass a test to get a license, then have years of on-the-job training. They begin each day with rounds, looking in on the animals and talking with keepers. They give checkups, clean teeth, and patch up injuries. Every day is different. They may visit an elephant about to have a baby, treat a frog with an eye infection, or examine a boa constrictor.

"We did . . . we tried. But then we heard voices. And we had to know what was going on."

"It's a good thing we did," Rosie continued. "Now we know those men stole the okapis and the other animals."

"What? How?" Ethan asked.

"They loaded them on a truck," Rosie continued. "Look, they wanted the zebras and monkeys also. They tried to break into the enclosures." She showed Ethan the grooves in the fences and the scratched-up locks. "They said they needed a bigger truck to get more animals tonight. They're going to try again. What can we do?"

"That doesn't make any sense, Rosie. We can't jump to conclusions," Ethan said.

Nodding, Ava agreed.

Rosie groaned. "You don't believe me!"

Ethan didn't answer. He was staring

at one of the puzzles. It was a Zebra Maze.

Zebra Maze

Help this zebra find the herd.

At the bottom of the page, Mr. Scott had listed zebra facts. The last one on the page said: "Zebras run and kick when they are scared. Instead of holding their ears straight up, they point them back."

Ethan gulped. He looked at the zebras, still racing around. He peered closer. Their ears *were* pushed back!

"Hmm, that may not be such a crazy story after all, Rosie," he said. He showed them their father's note about how zebras behave. "These zebras are acting scared. Maybe the men you saw *did* try to take them."

"Oh no!" Ava whispered, grabbing Rosie's hand. "And they already have those other animals. What about the mama pronghorn? The poor thing. She's having the babies soon."

"What should we do?" Rosie cried.

Ethan swallowed. He wasn't sure what was really going on. Who knew if there was even a real problem? He didn't want to worry his parents, but he decided to try to reach them. Ethan texted his dad: HEY DAD, WHEN WILL YOU BE BACK?

Ethan waited for an answer. But there was no response. *The meeting must still be happening,* he thought.

The sun was setting and the air was getting cool. Ethan was trying to figure out what to do. Just then the sound of a loud engine pierced the air.

CHAPTER 8

Unsolved Mystery

ROAR! BUZZ! BANG! CRASH!

"The truck," Ava gasped.

"They're back," Rosie hissed. "And it sounds like they have a really big truck now!"

Ethan, Rosie, and Ava stared in the direction of the woods. Then they looked around at the animals. They were acting more upset than ever.

The evening was growing darker.

"Okay." Ethan spoke softly and firmly. "Let's go back to the house and wait for Mom and Dad. C'mon."

"We have to save the animals," Rosie said, racing off toward the wooded area. Ava followed her twin sister. Ethan took off after them. His phone still in his hand, he turned on its flashlight to see in the darkened woods. Soon he caught up to Ava.

"Come on, Ethan," said Ava. "We have to catch up to Rosie."

They picked up speed. Leaves crunched with their every step. Suddenly, the machine noises stopped. Only Ethan's and Ava's footsteps echoed through the trees.

Where was Rosie now? Ethan held

up the cell phone flashlight. *There, by the boulder!* They sped up to keep her in sight, but then she disappeared.

"Where did she go?" said Ava. She and Ethan peered all around. They couldn't see Rosie anywhere.

Suddenly, a figure reached out and grabbed Ava's arm.

"Ahh!" she yelped.

"It's only me." Rosie giggled. Then she grew serious. "Let's be careful. The men are right on the other side of the fence."

The three siblings moved forward . . . slowly . . . quietly . . . until they reached the last tree before the fence.

Portable lights lit the road. They could see the men clearly now.

IF YOU'RE HAPPY AND YOU KNOW IT...

Most scientists agree: Just like humans, animals have feelings. Animals show their feelings with facial expressions, too. When chimpanzees are playing happily, they grin, showing all their teeth. What about when animals aren't happy? Gorillas bare their teeth when they feel angry. Alpacas spit. And many animals snarl.

HEY! Pay attention to me!

HAPPY! HAPPY! HAPPY!

TEE HEE! That tickles.

BACK OFF! I spit when I'm angry.

HELLO! I'm feeling friendly.

YAWN! I'm bored.

SNARL! I'm grumpy.

Ava took a deep breath. Rosie looked stunned. Ethan laughed.

"They're just construction workers!" Rosie said.

The men weren't trying to steal the animals. They were fixing the road.

"So then what happened to the missing animals?" Ava asked.

CHAPTER 9

Mystery Solved

For a moment, Ethan, Ava, and Rosie didn't move. Then Ethan's phone buzzed. He read his dad's text: WE GOT THE PERMIT. YAY!!! ON OUR WAY HOME.

The three kids hurried back to the cottage. Ethan noticed a neat stack of folders on the kitchen counter. "Isn't that just like Dad," he said to his sisters. Each folder was carefully labeled: "Camp Activities." "Snacks." "Animals."

Ava picked up the "Animals" folder. The top sheet listed all the zoo animals. "In alphabetical order, of course," Ava said. She went to the last page: "Zebra."

"Zebras are skittish prey animals," she read out loud. "They are hunted for food and easily scared."

"We already know that," Rosie said impatiently.

"When they are frightened, zebras feel stress," Ava went on. "One sign of zebras' stress is excessive chewing. Zebras may even bite enclosure bars."

"Those marks on the gates!" Rosie exclaimed.

Quickly, Ava flipped to "S" for "Squirrel Monkey." "Squirrel monkeys react strongly to any disturbance. In

ARE YOU UP?

Nocturnal means active at night. Some nocturnal animals—such as rabbits—sleep during the day to avoid predators searching for prey. Some—such as lions—are awake at night so they can hunt when it's cooler.

Diurnal animals are awake during the day. Humans, elephants, and gorillas are among the animals most active during the daytime. Some animals don't fall into either category. Deer, skunks, fireflies, and other *crepuscular* animals are most active during times of day when the light is dim—at dusk and just before dawn.

A herd of deer at dawn

NIGHT LIFE

Nocturnal animals have traits or abilities that help them get around in the dark. Rabbits have excellent hearing (those big ears). Many night hunters, including lions and owls, have eyes that help them see in the dark.

Snowy owl

stressful situations, they bite, bare their teeth, and make angry sounds."

Rosie snatched the sheet to read more. "Loud noises may be a cause."

"Like the construction," Ava put in.

"Stress causes odd behavior in okapis," Ethan read.

Quickly, Rosie thumbed through more pages, scattering papers everywhere. "Yup!" she said. "Tamarins don't like loud noises either."

"What do they do?" Ava asked.

"They hide."

Meanwhile, Ethan was looking up "P." "So do the pronghorns," he said.

"So the mama is hiding because she's scared," Ava put in. "She must be right there in the enclosure, we just couldn't see her."

"Mystery solved," Rosie said. "There must have been lots of construction noise when we were moving in to the cottage."

"But we couldn't hear it!" said Ava.

The siblings high-fived just as their parents walked in.

Mr. Scott eyed the papers all over the floor. "What happened here?" he asked.

"You'll never guess," Rosie said, bouncing up and down. "We have so much to tell you!"

The three took turns explaining. They told their parents about the "missing" animals. The teeth marks on the zebra gate. And the noisy construction that was scaring them all.

"That all makes sense," Mr. Scott agreed. "There was a detour sign on the side of the road when we drove back after the meeting."

"So the animals are fine," Mrs. Scott said with relief.

"No, they still need our help," Rosie insisted. "We have to go to the construction site to tell the men to stop. The zoo opens tomorrow—and the pronghorn's babies are due. The animals can't be upset and hiding now."

"You're absolutely right," said their dad. "Let's go!"

The family hurried to the site. "Excuse me!" Mrs. Scott waved her arms at the men, who were still

FAMILY TIME

Many animal families, like human families, live together and form strong bonds. Extended families of social animals such as lemurs and other primates may include aunts and uncles, too.

working. One by one, they turned off the drills and machines.

"Can I help you?" asked one man. The name "Ed" was stitched on his work jacket. "I'm the foreman."

"Yes, I hope you can, Ed," Mrs. Scott answered him.

Mr. and Mrs. Scott explained the situation. Ethan, Rosie, and Ava stood behind them, nodding.

Ed thought a moment. Then he said, "My crew can work farther down the road for now. At least for a week—we have a lot of repairs to do. We'll stay away from the zoo."

The children and their parents thanked the men. They would talk to Laura and figure out how to help the animals when the roadwork near the zoo was being completed.

As the Scotts walked back to the cottage, everyone was thinking the same thing. Would the animals have enough time to settle down for opening day? And would they come out of hiding for the campers and visitors?

"Night night, mama pronghorn," Ava whispered as they passed the animal's enclosure.

Opening Day!

The next morning, the twins woke early. They dressed quickly and went to check the animals. Outside, they came to the okapi enclosure first. The animals were grazing by the fence.

"Oh," Ava breathed a sigh of relief. "They're perfectly fine."

Then they checked the tamarins, and the pronghorns. All of the animals were out and about—they had settled down for opening day. The girls saw the vet at the pronghorn enclosure, and she told them that the babies would be born very soon. The sisters couldn't wait to tell their family the good news.

"Race you to the gate," Rosie said to Ava, and the girls took off.

Ava and Rosie arrived at the entrance just as Laura, their parents, and Ethan were greeting the first visitors: a man and woman with a boy and a girl around the twins' age.

"Welcome!" said Laura warmly.

"We're Mr. and Mrs. Turner," said the woman. "This is my daughter Sarah and her cousin Luke. They're here for zoo camp."

"We're so excited," said Sarah. She held out a blank notebook. "I'm going to fill this up with animal facts."

"You like to write?" Mrs. Scott asked Sarah. "I'm a writer, too."

Sarah nodded and smiled.

"Both Luke and Sarah have plenty of animal experience," said Mr. Turner. "They've worked on their grandparents' farm in Massachusetts. We're traveling cross-country to visit my other relatives."

"Well, I hope you don't mind being the star campers," Mr. Scott said with a nervous smile. "It looks like you're the only ones today."

Luke grinned. "That's okay. And I'm not lyin'. Get it? Lion?"

Sarah groaned. "Luke's used to people groaning at his lame jokes," she told Rosie and Ava.

"Let's get started," Mr. Scott said. "We're expecting pronghorn twins soon."

"Today! At least that's what the vet thinks," Laura added. "I called reporters at the TV station and newspaper this morning. They're on the way."

When Laura, Mr. Scott, and the others arrived at the pronghorn enclosure, they were bubbling with excitement. They called out to the vet, who waved and put a finger to her lips.

"Let's be quiet so we don't disturb mama pronghorn," Laura whispered.

Seconds later, two small, fuzzy pronghorn babies were born. Within minutes, they struggled to their feet and nuzzled their mother.

"They *are* twins!" Rosie cried at the sight of the sweet little babies. "They look exactly alike."

"Almost," Ava said, pointing to the babies. One had a small white patch of fur on its left side, and the other had a patch on its right side.

"Yeah! We'll be able to tell them apart," Sarah said, drawing a picture in her notebook. Luke and Ethan were excited, too.

Just then a group of reporters arrived, trailed by people toting equipment. Newspaper photographers snapped pictures. TV cameras filmed. The reporters walked around, taking notes. Mrs. Scott took notes, too. She planned to write about this amazing experience in her book.

"The babies are called fawns," Mr. Scott explained to everyone. "Pronghorns almost always have twins."

Laura pointed to Ava and Rosie. "Just like our very own set," she said, smiling.

"Let's get a shot of the human twins,

too," one reporter called out.

Rosie and Ava posed for the camera. Then Rosie gave the reporter a sheet of paper.

"It's a puzzle," she explained. "Solve it to find out the names we picked for the fawns."

Pronghorn Babies Rebus

Solve the puzzle to learn the babies' names.

- DE +   - SH +   - A

_____

- ALE +   - L + ER

_____

ZOO-LA-LA!

Some animals, such as snakes and lizards, are born ready to live on their own. But many baby animals need to learn how to be adults. Sometimes there isn't a mother or family to show them the way. Zookeepers look after these babies and teach them what they need to know to survive and thrive.

LOOKS LIKE MOM
A puppet helps an orphaned wattled crane baby learn to be an adult bird.

SWIM CLASS
A penguin chick gets a helping hand in the baby pool. Soon it will be ready to make waves on its own.

TABLE MANNERS

An orphaned sea otter needs to learn how to float and eat at the same time. That takes practice!

DOUBLE TROUBLE

This baby sloth is learning to hang upside down—while resting on its crib mate underneath.

GRADUATION

This baby gazelle was raised in a zoo nursery. Once it is used to the outdoor space, it will join the zoo herd.

"Great idea," the reporter said. She looked over the puzzle. "Skipper and Scamper. What great names. I can print this puzzle with my story."

"There are lots of other things going on here," Ethan chimed in, to everyone's surprise. "We're going to have a scavenger hunt. And a Puzzle Mania Contest," he added, sharing his new ideas for the zoo. The reporter jotted it all down for her story.

Laura smiled. It seemed that everyone was falling in love with her zoo.

The Scotts were up early on Day 2 of zoo camp. Mr. and Mrs. Scott were putting together animal fact sheets while the kids ate breakfast.

"We got great publicity yesterday," Ethan said, holding up the newspaper. "Rosie and Ava are on the front page of the *Fieldstone News*."

Ava and Rosie gasped. There they were, right next to a photo of the twin pronghorns.

"Look! You, too, Ethan," Rosie said, pointing at the TV on the counter. Ethan was on the early morning news.

The Scotts finished their preparations and headed to the zoo grounds. When they got to the gate, they saw a long line of people waiting for tickets.

"Whoa," Ethan said. "All right!"

Mr. Scott opened the gate, and people started pouring in.

Beaming, the twins handed out the fact sheets.

"Read all about it!" Rosie cried. "We're just like our animal friends! Find out how!"

"Wow!" said a teenager, reading the sheet. "Animals bite their nails when they're nervous." He looked at his own hand. "Like me before a test."

"Meet the animal expert," Rosie crowed. "My mom!" Immediately, a group crowded around Mrs. Scott.

"This is great," Laura said. "We have so many campers!"

"I can take a group," Ethan volunteered.

Mrs. Scott came over, smiling. "Whew! I've never answered so many questions!"

"Me, too," Mr. Scott said.

"This is amazing," Ethan said. "There are so many people. And look— there's Ed, the guy who helped us with the construction noise."

Ed waved and came over, holding a young girl's hand. "I just had to see for myself that the animals are fine," he explained. "Will there be a zoo camp over the summer, too? I'd love to sign up my daughter, Zoey."

"Well . . ." Laura began.

"We could stay!" Rosie interrupted.

"I'd like that." Ava nodded.

Mr. and Mrs. Scott looked at each other, then Mrs. Scott walked over to

Ethan. "What do you think about staying for the summer, Ethan?" she asked.

"Um," he said, hesitating. "I thought I'd be with my buddies back home for the summer."

"Ethan, look." Ava pointed out Laura's volunteers. They were all around Ethan's age. The girls and boys smiled and waved.

Ethan took a deep breath. "Okay," he said, gazing at the busy zoo. "New friends are good. Do you think the summer will be like this, too?"

"Yes! I'm so excited!" Rosie said, hopping up and down like a pronking pronghorn.

"No mystery there," Ava said with a smile.

Puzzle Solutions

PAGE 37
Unscramble #1:
Squirrel Monkey, Peccary.
Unscramble #2:
Capybara, Chinchilla.
Unscramble #3:
Rhinoceros Beetle,
Tarantula.

PAGE 42
Unscramble Bonus:
Okapi

PAGE 46

PAGE 47
Secret Bonus Word:
Tamarin

PAGE 55

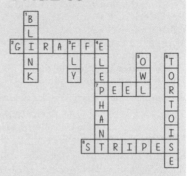

PAGE 75

PAGE 103
Skipper and Scamper

CREDITS AND ACKNOWLEDGMENTS

Writer Gail Herman
Illustrator Bryan Langdo
Produced by Scout Books & Media Inc
President and Project Director Susan Knopf
Editor Sonia Black
Managing Editor Brittany Gialanella
Copyeditor Stephanie Engel
Proofreader Peter Jaskowiak
Designer Annemarie Redmond

Advisor Michael Rentz, PhD, *Lecturer in Mammology, Iowa State University*

Thanks to the Time Inc. Books team: Margot Schupf, Anja Schmidt, Beth Sutinis, Deirdre Langeland, Georgia Morrissey, Megan Pearlman, Nina Reed, and Hillary Leary.

Special thanks to the Discovery and Animal Planet Creative and Licensing teams: Denny Chen, Carolann Dunn, Elizabeta Ealy, Summer Herrmann, Christina Lynch, Robert Marick, Doris Miller, and Janet Tsuei.

Photo Credits